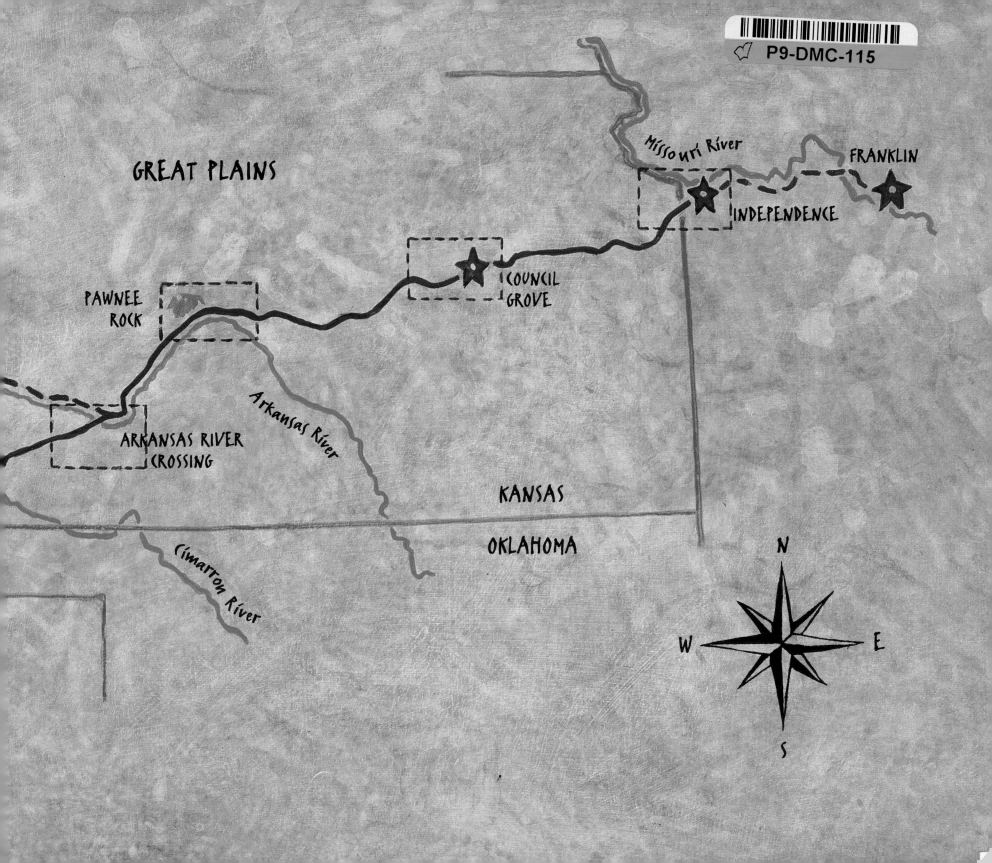

GREAT PLAINS

Missouri River

FRANKLIN

INDEPENDENCE

COUNCIL GROVE

PAWNEE ROCK

Arkansas River

ARKANSAS RIVER CROSSING

KANSAS

OKLAHOMA

Cimarron River

N
W   E
S

"For Nancy Hoppe, who took me
on another kind of trail. Thank you." —BJ

"To my twin brother, Daniel, who helped me
remember our childhood colors of the West." —JVZ

Text © 1998 by Barbara Joosse
Illustrations © 1998 by Jon Van Zyle

Book design by Vandy Ritter.
Typeset in Celestia Antiqua.
Printed in Hong Kong.

Library of Congress Information
Joosse, Barbara M.
Lewis and Papa *Adventure On the Santa Fe Trail* /
by Barbara Joosse ; illustrated by Jon Van Zyle.
p.   cm.
Summary: While accompanying his father
on the wagon train along the Santa Fe Trail,
Lewis discovers what it is to be a man.
ISBN 0-8118-1959-0
[1. Fathers and sons — Fiction. 2. Santa Fe Trail —
Fiction. 3. West (U.S.) — Fiction.]
I. Van Zyle, Jon, ill. II. Title.
PZ7.J74350n 1998
[E] – dc21   97-22572
CIP   AC

Distributed in Canada
by Raincoast Books
8680 Cambie Street
Vancouver B.C. V6P 6M9

10 9 8 7 6 5 4 3 2 1

Chronicle Books
85 Second Street
San Francisco, CA 94105

Web Site: www.chronbooks.com

LEWIS & PAPA

Adventure on the Santa Fe Trail

By Barbara Joosse

Illustrated by Jon Van Zyle

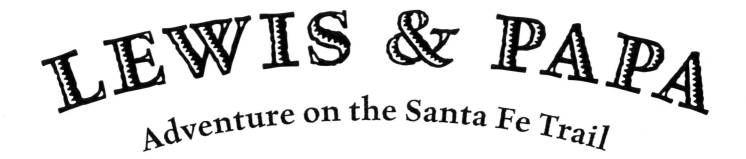

chronicle books · san francisco

ewis lived in a sturdy stone house on the Wisconsin River. One day a traveler happened by, and Papa invited him to spend the night. After stew and cornbread, the traveler spun stories about the Santa Fe Trail.

"The trail's so long, you leave a boy and come back a man. And hard. See this beard?" He spread out his white beard. "It was black as coal when I left," he said with a chuckle.

"But this here's the truth. In Santa Fe, they'll pay a pretty penny for goods from the East. My advice is to pack a wagon. In Santa Fe, you'll make your fortune."

After the man was asleep, Mama and Papa talked into the night. Lewis and Suzanna listened from the loft. Come spring, Papa would take the Santa Fe Trail. He'd take his favorite ox, Big Red, to pull the wagon. He'd take Lewis to help along the way.

It felt real nice that Papa wanted to take him. Made Lewis feel grown-up.

When spring broke the ice, and the apple trees filled with blossoms, Papa and Lewis packed to leave. Suzanna handed Lewis her lucky rock, the one smoothed by the river. Mama tucked some ginger snaps into Lewis' pocket and neatened his hair with her hand.

Lewis would really miss Mama! He'd miss Suzanna, too, and the river and the apples. Lewis' eyes filled with tears, but he hid his face so no one would see.

Independence, Missouri, was the gateway to the West. Boots, wheels, and hooves churned streets into mud. Cussing and gunfire crackled the air. Papa and Big Red weren't afraid, but Lewis was.

When it was time to load the wagon, Papa knew just how. "Heavy things on the bottom," he said, lifting the keg of nails. Lewis wondered if his muscles would ever bulge like Papa's. "Dry things at the top." Lewis scampered up with the calico and stuffed it into little crevices so the cloth would stay dry when they crossed the rivers. "Why, Lewis," Papa said, "you're as nimble as a cat."

The wagon groaned across the prairie. At night, Papa unhitched Big Red and the other oxen. He gave extra water to Big Red because he was his favorite.

The stars swept up in a great, wide arc. It made Lewis feel so small he thought he might disappear. In Council Grove, they would hook up with the rest of the wagon train. How long would it take to get to Santa Fe? Would they see Indians? Would they be friendly? Would there be wild animals? A coyote howled, and Lewis shivered.

"I never did like the sound of coyotes," said Papa, "but I feel right-brave next to you, Lewis."

At Council Grove, Lewis' stomach flip-flopped with excitement. When sixty men and forty wagons were in place, the wagon master blew his bugle. "Stretch out! Stretch out!" he cried. And they did. Forty prairie schooners, headed for Santa Fe.

Ahead lay more and more and more prairie. Papa was handy with a whip as he flicked the oxen into place. He never flicked Big Red though. He seemed to know what Papa wanted, and Papa rewarded him with pats on the flank.

Dark clouds of grasshoppers swelled before the oxen, and great, choking clouds of dust rose behind them. Lewis coughed from the dust. "Do you miss Mama?" Lewis asked.

"I surely do," Papa said, tying his kerchief across Lewis' mouth so the dust couldn't get in.

Santa Fe Trail

COUNCIL GROVE

At night, the wagons formed a circle. Papa covered Lewis with a buffalo robe and joined the other men around the campfire. Lewis wanted to stay up as long as Papa, but Big Red's slow breathing made his eyes heavy, and soon he was asleep.

Lewis woke up to a terrible thunder that shook the sky and the ground and everything on the prairie. The noise made Lewis' teeth chatter.

Papa's eyes flew open. "Buffalo!" he cried. The men drew their rifles, and Lewis made himself small under the wagon. Dust filled the sky until there was no blue. A shaggy-brown, thundering sea rolled in. The men began to shoot. The crack of their guns seemed small, not enough to stop the buffalo.

But when they came close, Papa stepped in front and shot. The lead bull collapsed and the herd parted around the wagon train.

Pawnee Rock

Santa Fe Trail

Arkansas River

That night, everyone feasted on "running meat" and told the story of Papa saving the wagon train. When they were settled under the wagon, Lewis said, "I was afraid when the buffalo came."

"So was I," said Papa. "My legs shook like Mama's grape jelly."

"But you stood in front anyway."

"I did what needed to be done. There's no shame in feeling scared."

At last the train reached the Arkansas River. There were steep banks and shifting sand! How would they get across?

The men cut down the bank with shovels. "I'll gather branches and shrubs," said Lewis. "We can throw them in the water so the oxen won't slide in the sand."

Lewis gathered as many branches as he could. "Lewis had a fine idea," one of the men said to Papa. "And he does a grown man's work."

Papa's chest swelled with pride, and he winked at Lewis. Then he filled the water barrels for the long, dry desert.

Mountain Branch

Arkansas River

Cimarron Cutoff

The desert was hot. The only water they had was in the barrels, so Lewis drank just a little.

Each day, Big Red became slower. Papa scraped a little more water out of the barrel, and Big Red drank it eagerly. Still, he hung his head in the heat. Then one afternoon the water ran out. Big Red's knees buckled, and he fell to the ground.

"Papa!" pleaded Lewis. "Do something!"

Papa put his big, callused hand on Lewis' shoulder. "There's nothing more I can do," said Papa. "And I can't let him suffer."

Papa patted Big Red lovingly and whispered something in his ear. He drew out his rifle, and Big Red raised his round eyes to him. Then Papa shot him.

No! Tears pushed at Lewis' eyes. He wanted Big Red back. He wanted Mama and her gingersnaps! But more than that, he wanted to be a man Papa would be proud of — a man who didn't cry — so he pushed his tears inside.

Papa wrapped his arms around Lewis, but Lewis brushed away. That's when he noticed something.

"Papa, you're crying!" he whispered.

"There's no shame in tears," said Papa. "Big Red and I have been together a long time. The shame would be in feeling nothing for such a good friend."

Lewis put his arm around Papa's big shoulders. Papa needed him now. He patted Papa's callused hand and cried with Papa until their tears were done.

The Santa Fe Trail was long and hard. And in the end, Lewis and Papa made a pretty penny. But the best part? They took the trail together. They dreamed under the stars and were thirsty under the sun. They did what needed to be done and cried when it was right.

And so it was that Papa taught Lewis to be a man...and Lewis taught Papa. And *that* was the real fortune.

SANTA FE

Sangre De Christo Mountains

Santa Fe Trail

THE SANTA FE TRAIL

1821-1880

900 miles, about 72 days

GREAT PLAINS

Missouri River

FRANKLIN

INDEPENDENCE

COUNCIL GROVE

PAWNEE ROCK

Mountain Branch

Arkansas River

ARKANSAS RIVER CROSSING

COLORADO

NEW MEXICO

KANSAS

OKLAHOMA

Cimarron Cutoff

Cimarron River

TEXAS

SANTA FE

N / S / E / W

Prior to 1821, Santa Fe was the northernmost capitol of new Spain, and trade from the U.S. was banned. Then in 1821, Mexico declared its independence, and foreign trade was welcome. The people in Santa Fe were anxious to buy goods from the East, and the Santa Fe Trail was born. This was a trade trail, not a settlement trail. So most of its travelers were men.

From Franklin, Missouri, to Santa Fe, New Mexico, the trail was long and hard. There were buffalo stampedes, Indian attacks, illness, and prairie fires.

But like the old traveler in this story said, you could make your fortune on the Santa Fe Trail. So bold men, willing to gamble their lives, packed their wagons full of merchandise to sell in Santa Fe.

Despite all the risks, it was the railroad that finally killed the Santa Fe Trail. In 1880, railroad tracks stretched from Missouri to New Mexico, and travel along the Santa Fe Trail ended. Today you can still walk in the ruts made by thousands of straining hoofs, bulging wagons, and booted heels.

Buffalo Also called bison, buffalo roamed the prairie freely, often in massive herds. When wood was scarce, buffalo chips could be burned for fuel.

Cimarron Cutoff A heartbreaking decision was made at the Arkansas River. Should the wagon train travel across the Colorado Rockies — adding one hundred wheel-breaking miles to the journey — or risk the shorter Cimarron Cutoff?

Council Grove, Kansas Nestled beside the Neosho River, and canopied by leafy shade on the otherwise tree-less prairie, Council Grove was the place where many wagon trains were formed. It was also the last place where hardwood could be found to mend a broken axle.

Independence, Missouri Spring was the wildest time of all in the "Gateway to the West." Melted snow turned the streets to mud. Excited travelers bought their wagons and supplies and packed them tight. In Independence Square, you could find traders, trappers, bullwhackers, muleskinners, Mexican herders, and French voyageurs.

Mules and Oxen Which was the better choice to pull a wagon — oxen or mule? Oxen were steadier, but slower, and could live off the land. Mules were faster, better for packtrains, but more willful.

Prairie Schooner Some people called the wagons "prairie schooners," because they looked like ships. Wagons were usually pulled by a dozen mules or six yoke of oxen.

Running Meat Because there was very little meat in a traveler's diet, freshly killed buffalo — "running meat" — was considered a delicacy.

Trade Goods Wagons were packed carefully — heavy things on the bottom, and calico on top, so it would stay dry when you crossed a river. Trade goods included: suspenders, ribbons, combs, needles, pocket knives, razors, china cups, nails, calico, wool, and earrings and brooches.

Wagon Train Prairie schooners traveled four wagons abreast, led by the wagon master, in groups known as wagon trains. At night, the trains formed a circle. Inside the circle, travelers swapped stories, sang, danced, and cooked their evening meal. They slept in the open or beneath the wagons.

A Note from the Author and the Artist

There's something called a picture book marriage — the quixotic union of author and illustrator in the making of a picture book. As in real life, there are lots of ways to make a bad picture book marriage. One of us can be too dominant. Or we can be too much alike. Sometimes, like in real life, we can be two good people who don't make magic happen.

If the best picture book marriage is between two strong and different individuals, Jon Van Zyle and I have a marriage made in heaven. I'm a little wordy. He's blunt. I paint with words, he with pictures. He races the Iditarod, finds cold bracing, *enjoys* eating trail food and sleeping on the ground, and I like...gardening.

I began to write this book because so many people wanted a story "like *Mama, Do You Love Me?* except for fathers." It was a good idea...but every quarter of every school year

I used to have one little box on my report card checked: *Does not follow instructions.* It wasn't long before I began asking the questions that would lead me away from the original idea. What's the nature of a father-son relationship? How are a boy's struggles to grow up different from a girl's? And finally — how does a boy learn of his father's love? Is it more by words or actions?

At the same time, my own son left on a backpacking trip with my husband. Rob came back less silly, less awkward, less of a boy and more of a man. But here's the part that really puzzled me — he returned with a sweetness and tenderness that had only been suggested before. So now there was another question. Why?

There's a moment in an author's life — the one we all crave — where questions and life experiences, images and metaphors suddenly collide and become a story. My desire to understand my son and his passage, my wish to chronicle this passage for other children, and my fascination with the Santa Fe Trail, became *Lewis & Papa: Adventure on the Santa Fe Trail*. The story took me over five years to write.

Next came the illustrations. Jon was not raised by a father. The story of the trail became incidental to him. The story Jon wanted to tell, through pictures, was the story of a father and son. Jon was able, in *Lewis & Papa*, to paint his own father into the picture.

Like a real union, a good picture book marriage is respectful — each of us leaves room for the other's creative breath. In the end, we hope our book, *Lewis & Papa: Adventure on the Santa Fe Trail*, is greater and stronger than either Jon or I could make alone.

THE SANTA FE TRAIL

1821 to 1880

Mountain Branch

COLORADO

NEW MEXICO

Cutoff

TEXAS

SANTA FE